T0132069

Lake, Sky, Dragonfly

by G.M. Ferrari
Illustrated by Mary Connors

AuthorHouse™
1663 Liberty Drive
Bloomington, IN 47403
www.authorhouse.com
Phone: 833-262-8899

Because of the dynamic nature of the Internet, any web addresses or links contained in this book may have changed since publication and may no longer be valid. The views expressed in this work are solely those of the author and do not necessarily reflect the views of the publisher, and the publisher hereby disclaims any responsibility for them.

Any people depicted in stock imagery provided by Getty Images are models, and such images are being used for illustrative purposes only.
Certain stock imagery © Getty Images.

This book is printed on acid-free paper.

ISBN: 978-1-4490-2895-4 (sc)
ISBN: 979-8-8230-2364-1 (e)

Print information available on the last page.

Published by AuthorHouse 03/07/2024

authorHOUSE

"Lake Life"

by G. M. Ferrari

It was too much for the Turtle family to take.
Tommy Turtle and his family had to move to the other side of the lake.
All the boats and the fishermen that came ...
Now this place will never be the same.

Freddie Fish never saw Tommy Turtle before.
And he knew everyone on this side of the shore.
The Turtle family moved in right next door.

Freddie Fish got excited about this because Tommy Turtle was his same size.
The fish around here were all too old and wise.

Freddie had a birthday just the other day.
The wish he made was for someone with whom he could play.
Now it seems his wish has come true.
Tommy Turtle would give him something to do.

But Freddie's father wouldn't let him go.
He said, "Fish and turtles are different, you know."
"You are a fish, and we have our pride!"
Freddie's father demanded he stay inside.

Freddie could not believe his ears.

And Freddie could not stop his tears.

He thought his father was very wrong.

Fish and turtles can get along!

They may look different, but that is okay.

It doesn't mean they cannot play.

Then Freddie Fish sneaked away.

His father's words he did not obey.

All he wanted to do was play.

Freddie Fish went to Turtle's house.

He and Tommy were quiet as a mouse.

They swam away to the other side

because to play together, they would have to hide.

But the other side of the lake is a dangerous place to be.

Fishing lines and hooks, to a fish, are not very friendly.

Just as things went terribly wrong,
that's when Freddie's father knew he was gone.
He began to panic and started to shake.
Could they really be on the other side of the lake?

Freddie thought the worm he saw would make a nice snack.
Then the SNACK bit him back!
The hook got Freddie, and it didn't look good.
But Tommy quickly snapped the line, 'cause he knew he could.

Tommy drags Freddie back home with the hook still in place.
Freddie's father sees the fear on his son's little face.
He gently takes out the hook.
Then he gives Tommy a grateful look.
"You saved my boy today,"
is what Freddie heard his father say.
"Tommy Turtle, you are welcome here anytime.
A friend of Freddie's is a friend of mine."

"The Unhappy Sky"

by G. M. Ferrari

Moon gets mad at Sun because Moon can only come out at night.
Clouds agree with Moon and they don't think Sun is right.
Clouds tell Moon that he should start a fight.

Moon gets Clouds to be mad at Sun too.
Sun is always telling them what to do.

Sun makes Clouds cover her every day.
Moon tells Clouds, "It shouldn't be that way."
Why should Sun always get her way?

Moon and Clouds make a deal.
The next time Sun starts to squeal,
calling Clouds to give her a rest,
They will hide way down low and Sun will have to continue her glow.

Moon said he could sleep all night and Sun would have to work hard to
    stay bright.
Moon and Clouds thought it would be funny
to force poor Sun to have to stay sunny.

After a few days of working all the time,
worn-out Sun loses her shine.
Sun falls right out of the sky.
Earth is now dark and doesn't know why.

Earth was scared and sad.
All this darkness was really bad.
No Sun to make the flowers grow.
No Moon to make the night glow.
No Clouds to give Sun rest.
Earth decides he better fix this mess.

Earth was loud when he spoke.
That's when Moon finally awoke.
Earth said, "Why do you sleep all the time?
Where have you been and why don't you shine?

"The night is yours, that's when you glow.
You light up my night and help me to show
all the wonderful places that my people can go."

Moon felt bad for letting Earth down.
It was really Sun that had made Moon frown.

Moon said sorry to Earth and explained why he went to sleep.
He said Sun was mean and made him weep.

Earth called Sun back to the sky.
Sun came running when she heard Earth's cry.
Earth said, "Why do you make Moon weep?"
Sun was ashamed and sank down deep.
Sun didn't know that Moon was so sad.
She did not mean to make him mad.

Sun thought things were going all right.
She liked shining all day while Moon shines all night.

She explained to Moon that she wanted to be fair.
Moon thought Sun just didn't care.
Earth asked for Sun and Moon to share.

Earth said, "You can share the sky."
Sun couldn't help but wonder why.
Why did Moon get so mad?
Why didn't he like the schedule they had?
He seems happy now, and yet the schedule is the same.
Could it be that Moon just likes to complain?
Maybe Moon shouldn't hang out with rain.

She is unhappy; all she does is cry.
You know, that's when water falls from the sky.

Sun wishes she could play with Moon.
But she knows that would bring the night too soon.

Clouds came back into the sky.
Sun waved as they floated by.
Clouds said, "Can't we just all get along?
Can't we try?"

So they all lived happily ever after.
The earth, the moon, the clouds, the sun.
Just one BIG HAPPY SKY!

Ladybug and Dragonfly
A Love Story

by G. M. Ferrari

Ladybug is busy sweeping. She knows Dragonfly is still sleeping. Ladybug keeps things neat. She wishes Dragonfly would wipe his feet. He always makes the biggest mess. She always cleans and never rests.

Dragonfly caught a bug for dinner, down by the water.
But Ladybug didn't want the dinner he brought her.

Dragonfly buzzes around her, trying to give her a kiss and a hug.
But this really annoys the Ladybug.

So they go for a little walk. They go past the old beanstalk.
Dragonfly loves to hear Ladybug talk.
Ladybug tells her tales of woe. She complains as they go.
Dragonfly knows she will never quit, but he doesn't mind one little bit.

Dragonfly loves her so and Ladybug doesn't seem to know.

They keep walking to the pond's edge. That's where Dragonfly makes
   his pledge.
He promised to always take care of Miss Ladybug.
He spread his wings and he gave her a hug.

A loud splash caught them both by surprise.

Neither one could believe their eyes.

A giant frog leaped out of the grass. Dragonfly knew he had to act fast.

Ladybug started to cry. With a broken wing, she could not fly.

Ladybugs are a tasty treat. They are a frog's favorite thing to eat.

Dragonfly flew into Frog's face, giving Ladybug time to get out of this place.

Frog's tongue came out with a loud snap. Dragonfly was now in a trap.

Frog was eating Dragonfly instead. Ladybug's best friend was dead.

Ladybug made her way back home. But no talking while walking; she was alone.

When Ladybug got up the next day, she told herself it would be okay.

She cried while she did her sweeping, for she knew Dragonfly was not just sleeping.

She misses the messes that he made and the kissing games he played.

She wishes she ate the dinner bugs. She wishes she accepted all of his hugs.

She misses their walking and wishes she didn't do all the talking.

Ladybug does love Dragonfly. She needs to tell him, she needs to try.
Ladybug shouts up toward the sky ...

"I LOVE YOU, DRAGONFLY!"

Ladybug wonders if he hears. She looks up through her tears.
She sees in the sky the brightest rainbows. That's how she knew
that Dragonfly knows ... she loved him.

Printed in the United States
by Baker & Taylor Publisher Services